Mommy's Lap

by
Ruth Horowitz

pictures by
Henri Sorensen

Lothrop, Lee & Shepard Books   New York

First Edition 1 2 3 4 5 6 7 8 9 10

Library of Congress Cataloging in Publication Data
Horowitz, Ruth. Mommy's lap / by Ruth Horowitz ; illustrated by Henri Sorensen.
p. cm. Summary: To Sophie's distress, her quiet times on Mommy's lap are
disrupted by the new baby growing inside Mommy, but once the baby arrives there is
room for Sophie on Mommy's lap again. ISBN 0-688-07235-6. — ISBN 0-688-07236-4
(lib. bdg.) [1. Babies—Fiction. 2. Brothers and sisters—Fiction.] I. Sorensen,
Henri, ill. II. Title. PZ7.H7877Mo 1991 [E]—dc20 90-32626 CIP AC

Printed in Hong Kong

For S.P.H.
—R.H.

For Nicola and her three sisters
—H.S.

Mommy's lap was the best place to be. Sophie loved to play there, and hear stories there, and sometimes fall asleep there.

Daddy's lap was fun to do tricks on. But Daddy's cheeks were too scratchy for nuzzling, and Daddy's knees were too bony for snuggling.

Grandma's lap was as soft as a pillow. But sometimes Grandma hugged too hard, and she told Sophie not to squirm. And Grandma wasn't Mommy.

Mommy's lap was just right. Sometimes Mommy held Sophie lightly, and sometimes she pulled her in tight for a squeeze. Mommy's lap was as snug as a warm slipper. And it was just the right size for Sophie.

But one day, Sophie noticed something was wrong. Mommy's lap didn't seem to be quite big enough anymore. "I'm getting bigger because there's a baby growing inside me!" Mommy said happily.

Daddy grinned. "Pretty soon you'll have a new little sister or brother."

Daddy wrapped his arms around Mommy, and Mommy smiled up at Daddy.

But Sophie didn't feel like smiling at anyone.

As the weeks passed, Mommy's lap got smaller and smaller.

Sophie wanted to snuggle up to Mommy. But Mommy said, "Sit here beside me and put your hand on my stomach. Maybe you'll feel the baby kick!"

Sophie tried to fix Mommy's hair. But Daddy said, "Mommy's too tired to play with you right now. Want to climb into my lap for a flip-flop?"

But Sophie wasn't in the mood for a flip-flop.

When Mommy came home, she was skinnier. The first thing she did was sit down in her favorite chair. Then Daddy handed her the baby. "And there's my Sophie," said Mommy. "Won't you give me a kiss? Come on over and say hello to baby Sam."

The baby was bundled in a soft yellow blanket, warm and snug and very small in Mommy's lap. Mommy smoothed the baby's bald head. Then she smiled at Sophie. "It's been a long time since I've held my big girl," she said. "I'll bet there's room for both of you on my lap. Let's see if we can move this little baby over."

Mommy settled the baby against one shoulder and wrapped her other arm around Sophie. Mommy's lap was soft, and warm, and very cozy for Sophie and the baby.

Now Sophie and Sam share Mommy's lap. Sometimes, Sophie has Mommy's lap all to herself. Sometimes, Mommy holds just the baby. And sometimes, when Mommy's very busy, she asks Sophie to hold the baby.

When Sophie holds the baby, she feels warm, and snug, and soft. Sometimes she even thinks her lap is the best place for baby Sam to be.

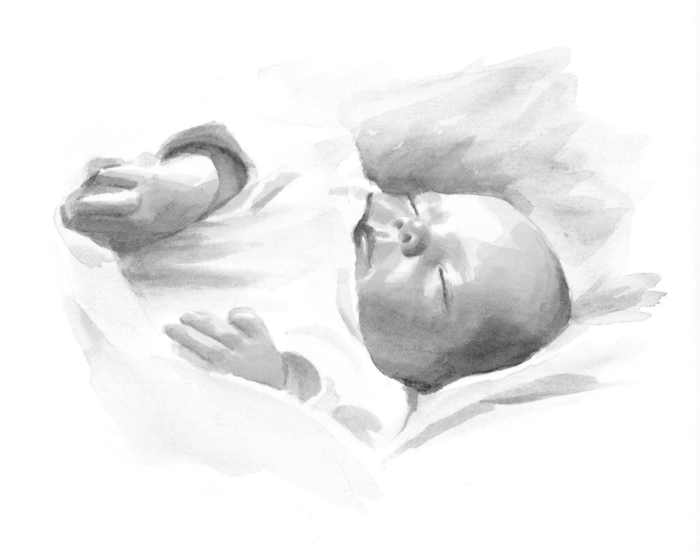